ROGER McGOUGH

Melting into the Foreground

VIKING

VIKING

Penguin Books Ltd, Harmondsworth, Middlesex, England
Viking Penguin Inc., 40 West 23rd Street, New York, New York 10010, U.S.A.
Penguin Books Australia Ltd, Ringwood, Victoria, Australia
Penguin Books Canada Limited, 2801 John Street, Markham, Ontario, Canada L3R 1B4
Penguin Books (N.Z.) Ltd, 182–190 Wairau Road, Auckland 10, New Zealand

This collection first published 1986
This collection copyright © Roger McGough, 1986

'A Crocodile in the City' was first published by The New Pyramid Press.
'The Boyhood of Raleigh' first appeared in *With a Poet's Eye*, published by the
Tate Gallery.

Typeset in Baskerville

Printed in Great Britain by
Richard Clay (The Chaucer Press) Ltd, Bungay, Suffolk

British Library Cataloguing in Publication Data

McGough, Roger
    Melting into the foreground.
    I. Title
    821'.914   PR6063.A219

ISBN 0-670-81289-7

Contents

Bye Bye Black Sheep

Volunteering at seventeen, Uncle Joe
Went to Dunkirk as a Royal Marine
And lived, not to tell the tale.
Demobbed, he brought back a broken 303,
A quiver of bayonets, and a kitbag
Of badges, bullets and swastikas
Which he doled out among warstruck nephews.

With gasflame-blue eyes and dark unruly hair
He could have been God's gift. Gone anywhere.
But a lifetime's excitement had been used up
On his one-and-only trip abroad. Instead,
Did the pools and horses. 'Lash me, I'm bored,'
He'd moan, and use language when Gran
Was out of the room. He was our hero.

But not for long. Apparently he was
No good. Couldn't hold down a job.
Gave the old buck to his Elders and Betters.
Lazy as sin, he turned to drink
And ended up marrying a Protestant.
A regular black sheep was Uncle Joe.
Funny how wrong kids can be.

Tramp Tramp Tramp

Insanity left him when he needed it most.
Forty years at Bryant & May, and a scroll
To prove it. Gold lettering, and a likeness
Of the Founder. Grandad's name writ small:
'William McGarry, faithful employee'.

A spent match by the time I knew him.
Choking on fish bones, talking to himself,
And walking round the block with a yardbrush
Over his shoulder. 'What for, Gran?' 'Hush . . .
Poor man, thinks he's marching off to war.

'Spitting image of Charlie, was your Grandad,
And taller too.' She'd sigh. 'Best-looking
Man in Seaforth. And straight-backed?
Why, he'd walk down Bridge Road
As if he had a coat-hanger in his suit.'

St Joseph's Hospice for the Dying, in Kirkdale,
Is where Chaplin made his last movie.
He played Grandad, and gave a fine performance
Of a man raging against God, and cursing
Nuns and nurses who tried to hold him down.

Insanity left him when he needed it most.
The pillow taken from his face
At the moment of going under. Screaming
And fighting to regain the years denied,
His heart gave out, his mind gave in, he died.

The final scene brings tears to everybody's eyes.
In the parlour, among suppurating candles
And severed flowers, I see him smiling
Like I'd never seen him smile before.
Coat-hanger at his back. Marching off to war.

Hearts and Flowers

                       Aunty Marge,
Spinster of the parish, never had a boyfriend.
Never courted, never kissed.
A jerrybuilt dentist and a smashed jaw
Saw to that.

                          To her,
Life was a storm in a holy-water font
Across which she breezed
With all the grace and charm
Of a giraffe learning to windsurf.

                      But sweating
In the convent laundry, she would iron
Amices, albs and surplices
With such tenderness and care
You'd think priests were still inside.

                      Deep down,
She would like to have been a nun
And talked of missing her vocation
As if it were the last bus home:
'It passed me by when I was looking the other way.'

                          'Besides,'
She'd say, 'What Order would have me?
The Little Daughters of the Woodbine?
The Holy Whist Sisters?' A glance at the ceiling.
'He's not that hard up.'

                            We'd laugh
And protest, knowing in our hearts that He wasn't.
But for the face she would have been out there,
Married, five kids, another on the way.
Celibacy a gift unearned, unasked for.

                But though
A goose among grown-ups,
Let loose among kids
She was an exploding fireworks factory,
A runaway pantomime horse.

                 Everybody's
Favourite aunt. A cuddly toy adult
That sang loud and out of tune.
That dropped, knocked over and bumped into things,
That got ticked off just like us.

                                    Next to
A game of cards she liked babysitting best.
Once the parents were out of the way
It was every child for itself. In charge,
Aunt Marge, renegade toddler-in-chief.

                                    Falling
Asleep over pontoon, my sister and I,
Red-eyed, would beg to be taken to bed.
'Just one more game of snap,' she'd plead,
And magic two toffees from behind an ear.

                          Then suddenly
Whooshed upstairs in the time it takes
To open the front door. Leaving us to possum,
She'd tiptoe down with the fortnightly fib:
'Still fast asleep, not a murmur all night. Little angels.'

                                    But angels
Unangelic, grew up and flew away. And fallen,
Looked for brighter toys. Each Christmas sent a card
With kisses, and wondered how she coped alone.
Up there in a council flat. No phone.

                    Her death
Was as quick as it was clumsy. Neighbours
Found the body, not us. Sitting there for days
Stiff in Sunday best. Coat half-buttoned, hat askew.
On her way to Mass. Late as usual.

                        Her rosary
Had snapped with the pain, the decades spilling,
Black beads trailing. The crucifix still
Clenched in her fist. Middle finger broken.
Branded into dead flesh, the sign of the cross.

                    From the missal
In her lap, holy pictures, like playing cards,
Lay scattered. Five were face-up:
A Full House of Sacred Hearts and Little Flowers.
Aunty Marge, lucky in cards.

Bars are Down

When I was a lad
most people round our way
were barzydown.

It was a world full of piecans.
Men who were barmy, married to women
who wanted their heads examined.

When not painting the railings,
our neighbours were doolally,
away for slates.

Or so my dad reckoned.
Needed locking away
the lot of them.

Leaving certain McGoughs
and a few close friends
free to walk the empty streets

in peace. Knowing exactly
whether we were coming or going.
Self-righteous in polished shoes.

Picking our way
clearheadedly,
between loose screws.

Here I Am

Here I am
forty-seven years of age
and never having gone to work in ladies' underwear

Never run naked at night in the rain
Made love to a girl I'd just met on a plane

At that awkward age now between birth and death
I think of all the outrages unperpetrated
            opportunities missed

                The dragons unchased
                The maidens unkissed
                The wines still untasted
                The oceans uncrossed
                The fantasies wasted
                The mad urges lost

            Here I am
            getting on for seventy
and never having stepped outside for a fight

Crossed on red, pissed on rosé (or white)
Pretty dull for a poet, I suppose, eh? Quite.

Today is Not a Day for Adultery

Today is not a day for adultery.
The sky is a wet blanket
Being shaken in anger. Thunder
Rumbles through the streets
Like malicious gossip.

Take my advice: braving
The storm will not impress your lover
When you turn up at the house
In an anorak. Wellingtons,
Even coloured, seldom arouse.

Your umbrella will leave a tell-tale
Puddle in the hall. Another stain
To be explained away. Stay in,
Keep your mucus to yourself.
Today is not a day for sin.

Best pick up the phone and cancel.
Postpone until the weather clears.
No point in getting soaked through.
At your age, a fuck's not worth
The chance of catching 'flu.

Prayer to Saint Grobianus

The patron saint of coarse people

Intercede for us dear saint we beseech thee
 We fuzzdutties and cullions
 Dunderwhelps and trollybags
 Lobcocks and loobies.

On our behalf seek divine forgiveness for
 We puzzlepates and pigsconces
 Ninnyhammers and humgruffins
 Gossoons and clapperdudgeons.

Have pity on we poor wretched sinners
 We blatherskites and lopdoodles
 Lickspiggots and clinchpoops
 Quibberdicks and Quakebuttocks.

Free us from the sorrows of this world
And grant eternal happiness in the next
 We snollygosters and gundyguts
 Gongoozlers and groutheads
 Ploots, quoobs, lurds and swillbellies.

As it was in the beginning, is now, and ever shall be,
World without end. OK?

Poem with a Limp

Woke up this morning with a
                              limp.
Was it from playing
                    football
In my dreams? Arthrite's first
                              arrow?
Polio? Muscular dystrophy? (A bit of
                                    each?)

I staggered around the kitchen spilling
                                        coffee
Before hobbling to the bank for
                                lire
For the holiday I knew I would not be
                                      taking.
(For Portofino read Stoke
                          Mandeville.)

Confined to a wheelchair for the
                                  remainder
Of my short and tragic life.
                              Wheeled
On stage to read my terse, honest
                                  poems
Without a trace of bitterness. 'How
                                    brave.

And smiling still, despite the
                              pain.'
Resigned now to a life of quiet
                              fortitude
I plan the nurses' audition.
                              Mid-afternoon
Sees me in the garden, sunning my
                              limp.

*   *   *

It feels a little easier now.
Perhaps a miracle is on its way?
(Lourdes, WII.)

By opening-time the cure is complete.
I rise from my deck-chair:
'Look, everybody, I can walk, I can walk.'

Bits of Me

When people ask: 'How are you?'
I say, 'Bits of me are fine.'
And they are. Lots of me I'd take
anywhere. Be proud to show off.

But it's the bits that can't be seen
that worry. The boys in the backroom
who never get introduced.
The ones with the Latin names

who grumble about the hours I keep
and bang on the ceiling
when I'm enjoying myself. The overseers.
The smug biders of time.

Over the years our lifestyles
have become incompatible.
We were never really suited
and now I think they want out.

One day, on cue, they'll down tools.
Then it's curtains for me. (Washable
plastic on three sides.) Post-op.
Pre-med. The bed nearest the door.

Enter cheerful staff nurse (Irish
preferably), 'And how are you today?'
(I see red.) Famous last words:
'Bits of me are fine.' On cue, dead.

Worry

Where would we be without worry?
It helps keep the brain occupied.
Doing doesn't take your mind off things,
I've tried.

Worry is God's gift to the listless.
Best if kept bottled inside.
I once knew a man who couldn't care less.
He died.

Melting into the Foreground

Head down and it's into the hangover.
Last night was a night best forgotten.
(Did you really kiss a man on the forehead?)

At first you were fine.
Melting into the foreground.
Unassuming. A good listener.

But listeners are speakers
Gagged by shyness
And soon the wine has
Pushed its velvet fingers down your throat.

You should have left then. Got your coat.
But no. You had the Taste.
Your newfound gift of garbled tongue
Seemed far too good to waste.

Like a vacuum-cleaner on heat
You careered hither and thither
Sucking up the smithereens
Of half-digested chat.

When not providing the lulls in conversation
Your strangled banter
Stumbled on to disbelieving ears.

Girls braved your leering incoherences
Being too polite to mock
(Although your charm was halitoxic,
Your wit, wet sand in a sock).

When not fawning over the hostess
You were falling over the furniture
(Helped to your feet, I recall,
By the man with the forehead).

Gauche attempts to prise telephone numbers
From happily married ladies
Did not go unnoticed.

Nor did pocketing a bottle of Bacardi
When trying to leave
In the best coat you could find.

I'd lie low if I were you.
Stay at home for a year or two.
Take up painting. Do something ceramic.
Failing that, emigrate to somewhere Islamic.

The best of luck whatever you do.
I'm baling out, you're on your own.
Cockpit blazing, out of control,
Into the hangover. Head down.

Trees Cannot Name the Seasons

Trees cannot name the seasons
Nor flowers tell the time.
But when the sun shines
And they are charged with light,
They take a day-long breath.
What we call 'night'
Is their soft exhalation.

And when joints creak yet again
And the dead skin of leaves falls,
Trees don't complain
Nor mourn the passing of hours.
What we call 'winter'
Is simply hibernation.

And as continuation
Comes to them as no surprise
They feel no need
To divide and itemize.
Nature has never needed reasons
For flowers to tell the time
Or trees put a name to seasons.

Conservation Piece

The countryside must be preserved!
(Preferably miles away from me.)
Neat hectares of the stuff reserved
For those in need of flower or tree.

I'll make do with landscape painting
Film documentaries on TV.
And when I need to escape, panting,
Then open-mouthed I'll head for the sea.

Let others stroll and take their leisure,
In grasses wade up to their knees,
For I derive no earthly pleasure
From the green green rash that makes me sneeze.

Green Piece

Show me a salad
    and I'll show you a sneeze
Anything green
    makes me weak at the knees
On St Patrick's day
    I stay home and wheeze
I have hay fever all the year round.

Broken-down lawnmowers
    Bring me out in a sweat
A still-life of flowers,
    in oils, and I get
All the sodden signs
    of a sinus upset
I have hay fever all the year round.

A chorus of birdsong
    makes my flesh creep
I dream of a picnic
    and scratch in my sleep
Counting pollen
    instead of sheep
I have hay fever all the year round.

Summertime's great
    (except for the sun)
Holly and mistletoe
    make my nose run
Autumn leaves and I swoon
    it's no fun
Having hay fever all the year round.

First Haiku of Spring

	cuck	oo	cuck	oo	cuck	
oo	cuck	oo	cuck	oo	cuck	oo
	cuck	oo	cuck	oo	cuck	

Sap

Spring again.
No denying the signs.
Rates bill. Crocuses on cue.
Daffodils rearing up
Like golden puff-adders.

Open to the neck, voices
Are louder. Unmuffled.
The lid lifted off the sky.
In the air, suddenly,
A feeling of *'je sais quoi'*.

I take the dog into the park.
Let myself off the lead.

Malteasers

Twelve Holiday snapshots

(i)   Xaghra:
        The sun
        behind you
        jaws open

(ii)   Zurrieq:
        village square
        noon. You
        and your shadow
        posing

(iii)   Mosta:
        after noon
        Your shadow
        posing.
        In the distance
        You
        sitting it out

(iv)   Golden Bay:
        a white sticky hand
        melting
        holds an empty
        ice-cream cone

(v)   Ghajn Tuffieha:
Turkish kids
laying siege
to Maltese
sandcastles

(vi)   Birzebbuga:
the shadow
of an ice-cream cone
sticky and melting
seeps
into the sand

(vii)   Valletta:
a Liberian tanker
laden
with suntan oil
slides
into the harbour.
Slickly

(viii)   Mgarr
is bzarr
Valletta
is betta

(ix)   Baya:
The Bay of Nuns.
Mermaids of the Lord
wearing black bivouacs
frolic piously
in the foam

(x)   Victoria:
in the bar
at lunchtime
topless
Gozo dancers

(xi)   Dwejra:
neolithic railway lines
reach out to Sicily.
In the depot on the seafloor
stone locomotives
await the seismic recall
to service

(xii)   Breakfast at Birgu
Sliema lunch date
Tea at Tarxien
Mdina at eight.

What prevents a poem
from stretching into Infinity?

what prevents a poem
from stretching into Infinity
is the invisible frame
of its self-imposed concinnity

The Boyhood of Raleigh

After the painting by Millais

Entranced, he listens to salty tales
Of derring-do and giant whales,

Uncharted seas and Spanish gold,
Tempests raging, pirates bold.

And his friend? 'God, I'm bored.
As for Jolly Jack I don't believe a word.

What a way to spend the afternoons –
the stink of fish, and those ghastly pantaloons!'

From 'Les Pensées'
by Le Duc de Maxim

Beside the willowèd river bank
Repose I, still and thinking,
When into the water fall a man
Who fast begin the sinking.

Chance at last to test
A maxim, so unblinking,
I toss to him the straw
Through which I drinking.

Sure enough, he clutch the straw
And scream, alas in vain.
He grasp until he gasp his last
And all is peace again.

Homewardly I pensive trek
Impatient now to note
How the fingers of the sun
Did linger on his throat.

And how he sank, and how
The straw continuèd to float,
'How wise the age-old axioms,
And yet how sad,' I wrote.

For Want of a
Better Title

The Countess
when the Count passed away

During a Bach
cello recital

Married an Archduke
the following day

For want of a better title.

How Patrick Hughes
Got to be Taller

Patrick was always taller.
In Bradford
when he drove a brick wall
and grew prize rainbows
he certainly was.

One of his secrets
is self-portraiture.
He draws himself
up to his full height
then adds a few inches
for good measure.

Another is his ability
to reduce the scale of objects
and people around him.

While friends and I
shrink into middle age
Patrick, cock-a-snook,
stands out like a tall thumb
on the nose of time.

Evenings I see him,
perspected against the bar
Full of *trompe-l'œil*
Beer in hand
Taller.

Who Can Remember Emily Frying?

The Grand Old Duke of Wellington
Gave us the wellington boot.
The Earl of Sandwich, so they say,
Invented the sandwich. The suit

Blues saxophonists choose to wear
Is called after Zoot Sims (a Zoot suit).
And the inventor of the saxophone?
Mr Sax, of course. (Toot! Toot!)

And we all recall, no trouble at all,
That buccaneer, long since gone,
Famed for his one-legged underpants –
'Why, shiver me timbers' – Long John.

But who can remember Emily Frying?
(Forgotten, not being a man.)
For she it was who invented
The household frying pan.

And what about Hilary Teapot?
And her cousin, Charlotte Garden-Hose?
Who invented things to go inside birdcages
(You know, for budgies to swing on). Those.

Good Old William

'I concur
with everything you say,'
smiled William.

'Oh yes,
I concur with that,
I agree.'

'If that's the general feeling
You can count on me.
Can't say fairer.'

Good old
William, the Concurrer.

low jinks

today
i will play low jinks,
be commonplace.

will merge,
blend, change
not one jot.

be beige, be –
have, my friend
will fault me not.

couching myself
in low terms
i will understate.

today
i will give the little blue ones a miss,
and see what happens.

The Filmmaker
(with subtitles)

He was a filmmaker with a capital F.
Iconoclastic. He said 'Non' to Hollywood,   1
'Pourquoi? Ici je suis Le Chef.'   2
A director's director. Difficult but good.

But when Mademoiselle La Grande C.   3
Crept into his bed in Montparnasse
And kissed him on the rectum, he
Had a rectumectomy. But in vain. Hélas.   4

And how they mourned, the aficionados.
(Even stars he'd not met were seen to grieve,
The Christies, Fondas, Streeps and Bardots.)
And for them all, he'd one last trick up his sleeve.

'Cimetière Vérité' he called it (a final pun).   5
In a fashionable graveyard in Paris 3ième.
He was buried, and at the going down of the sun
Premiered his masterpiece, *La Mort, C'est Moi-même.*   6

The coffin, an oblong, lead-lined studio with space
For the body, a camera and enough light
To film in close-up that once sanguine face
Which fills the monumental screen each night.

The show is 'Un grand succès'. People never tire   7
Of filing past. And in reverential tone
They discuss the symbolism, and admire
Its honesty. *La Vérité* pared down to the bone.   8

FIN   9

1 'No.'   2 'Why? Here I am the chef.'   3 Miss the Big C.
4 Alas.   5 'True cemetery'   6 *The Death it is Myself.*
7 'A grand success'.   8 The Truth   9 End

The Host

He can sing and dance
Play piano, trumpet and guitar.
An amateur hypnotist
A passable ventriloquist
Can even walk a tightrope
(But not far). When contracted,
Can lend a hand to sleight-of
And juggling. Has never acted,
But is, none the less, a Star.

He has a young wife. His third.
(Ex-au pair and former
Swedish Beauty Queen)
And an ideal home
In the ideal home counties.
His friends are household
Names of stage and screen,
And his hobbies are golf,
And helping children of those
Less fortunate than himself
Get to the seaside.

Having been born again. And again.
He believes in God. And God
Certainly believes in him.
Each night before going to bed
He kneels in his den
And says a little prayer:
'Thank you Lord, for my work and play,
Please help me make it in the U.S.A.'

Then still kneeling, with head bowed,
He tries out new material
(Cleaned up, but only slightly).
And the Almighty laughs out loud
Especially at jokes about rabbis
And the Pope. Just one encore
Then time for beddy-byes.
So he stands, and he bows,
Blows a kiss to his Saviour,
Then dances upstairs to divide Scandinavia.

Ode on a Danish Lager

The finger
enters the ring. A
pplause. Hooray!
Unzip.   A
pause. Then, whoosh,
The golden spray.

Unfurling slowly
like a blue mist
from a sorcerer's cave,
the genie is released
to serve a master
(soon to be slave).

A sip to mull over
the flavour
found only in the first.
I make a wish,
then slake
an imaginary thirst.

I squeeze the can
(it is not cannish),
is yielding, unmanish.
In it, my reflection,
modiglianish.

We wink at each other,
We're getting on well,
The genie weaves
his genial spell.

I unmask one more
(unheed the body's warning).
Goodnight, sweet beer,
See you in the morning!

Breakfast near Tiffany's

orange juice scrambled
over-easy followed
by New Jersey-bred
duck-flavoured bacon
with choice of either
coffee or unlimited
abuse. $3.95.

Muffin the Cat

Written at the Arvon Foundation,
Lumb Bank, Yorkshire

I had never considered cats
until Nadia said I should:
'If a person likes a cat,
then that person must be nice.'
So I seized the chance to be good
by taking her advice.

When Muffin (not the mule) called
around midnight to inspect the room
I was, at first, distinctly cool.
Until, remembering the New Me,
I praised felinity and made tea.
Offered him a biscuit. A cigarette.
Tried to make conversation.
He'd not be drawn. Not beaten yet
I showed him my collection
of Yugoslavian beermats.
He was unimpressed. (Queer, cats.)

At 2 a.m. I got out the whisky.
He turned up his nose.
After a few glasses I told him
about the problems at home.
The job. My soul I laid bare.
And all he did was stare.

Curled up on the duvet
with that cat-like expression.
Not a nod of encouragement.
Not a mew. Imagine the scene;
I felt like that intruder
on the bed with the Queen.

But I soldiered on till morning
and despite his constant yawning
told him what was wrong with the country.
The class system, nuclear disarmament,
the unions, free-range eggs.
I don't know what time he left.
I fell asleep. Woke up at four
With a hangover the size of a Yorkshire Moor.
And my tongue (dare I say it?) furry.

Since then, whenever I see the damn thing
He's away up the mountain to hide.
And I was only being friendly.
I tried, Nadia, I tried.

Q

I join the queue
We move up nicely.

I ask the lady in front
What are we queuing for.
'To join another queue,'
She explains.

'How pointless,' I say,
'I'm leaving.' She points
To another long queue.
'Then you must get in line.'

I join the queue.
We move up nicely.

Happy Birthday

One morning as you step out of the bath
The telephone rings.
Wrapped loosely in a towel you answer it.

As you pick up the receiver
The front doorbell rings.
You ask the caller to hang on.

Going quickly into the hall
You open the door the merest fraction.
On the doorstep is a pleasing stranger.

'Would you mind waiting?' You explain,
'I'm on the telephone.' Closing the door to,
You hurry back to take the call.

The person at the other end is singing:
'Happy Birthday to you, Happy Birthday . . .'
You hear the front door click shut.

Footsteps in the hall.
You turn . . .

Laughing, all the way to Bank

The beautiful girl
in the flowing white dress
struggled along the platform
at the Angel.

In one hand
she carried a large suitcase.
In the other, another.

On reaching me
she stopped. Green eyes flashing
like stolen butterflies.

'Would you be so kind
as to carry one for me,'
she asked, 'as far as Bank?'

I laughed: 'My pleasure.'
And it was. Safe from harm,
All the way to Bank,
Moist in my palm, one green eye.

All Over bar the Shouting

It's all over.
Almost a bar-room brawl.

Shouting does not become you.
Becomes you not at all.

It becomes me.
Shouting becomes me.

I become shouting.
I shout and shout and shout.

I shout until shouting
and I are one.

You walk out.
Leave me lock-

jawed in shout.
Dumbstuck.

Into the bar
the ghosts of years come streaming.

It's all over,
bar the shouting. Bar the screaming.

Last Lullaby

The wind is howling,
    My handsome, my darling,
An illwisher loiters
    Outside in the street.
The pain in your breastbone
    Tightens and tightens
And you are alone,
    My treasure, my sweet.

Gone is your lover,
    My angel, my dearest,
Gone to another
    To hold and caress.
Could that shadow you see
    On the curtain be me?
Of course not, beloved,
    Goodnight and God bless.

Are they not gentle,
    My naughty, my precious,
These hands that will bring you
    To sleep by and by?
Sweet dreams, my sweetheart,
    Hush, don't you cry.
Daddy will sing you
    A last lullaby.

Daddy will sing you
    A last lullaby.

My Little Eye

The cord of my new dressing-gown
he helps me tie

Then on to my father's shoulder
held high

The world at night with my little eye
I spy

The moon close enough to touch
I try

Unheard of silver elephants have learned
to fly

Giants fence with searchlights
in the sky

Too soon into the magic shelter
he and I

Air raids are so much fun
I wonder why

In the bunk below, a big boy
starts to cry.

A Joy to be Old

It's a joy to be old.
Kids through school,
The dog dead and the car sold.

Worth their weight in gold,
Bus passes. Let asses rule.
It's a joy to be old.

The library when it's cold.
Immune from ridicule.
The dog dead and the car sold.

Time now to be bold.
Skinnydipping in the pool.
It's a joy to be old.

Death cannot be cajoled.
No rewinding the spool.
The dog dead and the car sold.

Get out and get arse'oled.
Have fun playing the fool.
It's a joy to be old.
The dog dead and the car sold.

In Transit

She spends her life
in Departure Lounges,
flying from one to another.

Although planes frighten her,
baggage is a bother
and foreigners a bore,

in the stifled hysteria
of an airport
she, in transit, feels secure.

Enjoys the waiting game.
Cheered by storms, strikes
and news of long delays,

among strangers, nervous
and impatient for the off,
the old lady scrambles her days.

Wheelchairs

After a poetry reading at a geriatric
hospital in Birmingham, December 1983

I go home by train
with a cig and a Carly.
Back at the gig
the punters, in bed early
dither between sleep and pain:
'Who were those people?
What were they talking?'

The staff,
thankful for the break,
the cultural intrusion,
wheel out the sherry
and pies. Look forward
to a merry Christmas
and another year of caring
without scrutiny.

Mutiny!
In a corner,
the wheelchairs,
vacated now, are cooling.
In the privacy of darkness
and drying piss,
sullen-backed,
alone at last,
they hiss.

On the Road

Getting on at Notting Hill
A baglady. More or less.
Big, sad and grey.
Late thirties at a guess.

Change at Euston
for the Marrakesh Express.
Elastic-band bangles,
sandal-length dress.

Layer upon layer
of embroidered tat.
Smoke-blackened mirrors,
large floppy hat.

A mucky pup
(Afghan hound?)
in hippy best.
(Morocco bound

with Crosby, Stills and Hope.)
Lamour?
Whatever happened
to l'amour?

Kohl-black eyes downcast
flutter now and then
at men who fast
avert their gaze.

Neil Young, where art thou now?
Donovan, T. Rex?
Those incensesensual days,
Sweet nights of sex.

She puffs hard her cigarette,
Lets loose the ash.
Dreams about l'amour
and Graham Nash.

A Fair Day's Fiddle

Why can't the poor have the decency
to go around in bare feet?
Where's the pride that allows them
to fall behind on video recorders?

Such ostentation's indiscreet
when we can hardly afford as
much. They all smoke, of course,
and fiddle while the nation burns.

(Electric meters usually, and gas.)
And note, most have central heating.
Moonlighting's too romantic a word
for what's tantamount to cheating.

It's a question of priorities, I suppose,
give them money and it goes on booze.
Why can't the poor be seen to be poor?
Then we could praise the Lord, and give them shoes.

The Jogger's Song

After leaving the Harp nightclub in Deptford, a 35-year-old woman was raped and assaulted by two men in Fordham Park. Left in a shocked and dishevelled state she appealed for help to a man in a light-coloured track-suit who was out jogging. Instead of rescuing her, he also raped her.

Standard, 27 January 1984

Well, she was asking for it.
Lyin there, cryin out,
dyin for it. Pissed of course.
Of course, nice girls don't.
Don't know who she was,
where from, didn't care.
Nor did she. Slut. Slut.

Now I look after myself. Fit.
Keep myself fit. Got
a good body. Good body. Slim.
Go to the gym. Keep in trim.
Girls like a man wiv a good body.
Strong arms, tight arse. Right
tart she was. Slut. Pissed.

Now I don't drink. No fear.
Like to keep a clear
head. Keep ahead. Like
I said, like to know what I'm doin
who I'm screwin (excuse language).
Not like her. Baggage. Half-
dressed, couldn't-care-less. Pissed.

Crawlin round beggin for it.
Lyin there, dyin for it.
Cryin. Cryin. Nice girls don't.
Right one she was. A raver.
At night, after dark,
on her own, in the park?
Well, do me a favour.

And tell me this:
If she didn't enjoy it,
why didn't she scream?

The End of Summer

It is the end of summer
The end of day and cool,
As children, holiday-sated,
Idle happily home from school.
Dusk is slow to gather
The pavements still are bright,
It is the end of summer
And a bag of dynamite

Is pushed behind the counter
Of a department store, and soon
A trembling hand will put an end
To an English afternoon.
The sun on rooftops gleaming
Underlines the need to kill,
It is the end of summer
And all is cool, and still.

A Cautionary Calendar

Beware January,
His greeting is a grey chill.
Dark stranger. First in at the kill.
Get out while you can.

Beware February,
Jolly snowman. But beneath the snow
A grinning skeleton, a scarecrow.
Don't be drawn into that web.

Beware March,
Mad Piper in a many-coloured coat
Who will play a jig then rip your throat.
If you leave home, don't go far.

Beware April,
Who sucks eggs and tramples nests.
From the wind that molests
There is no escape.

Beware May,
Darling scalpel, gall and wormwood.
Scented blossom hides the smell
Of blood. Keep away.

Beware June,
Black lipstick, bruise-coloured rouge,
Sirensong and subterfuge.
    The wide-eyed crazed hypnotic moon.

Beware July,
Its juices overflow. Lover of excess
Overripe in flyblown dress.
    Insatiable and cruel.

Beware August,
The finger that will scorch and blind
Also beckons. The only place you will find
    To cool off is the morgue.

Beware September,
Who speaks softly with honeyed breath.
You promise fruitfulness. But death
    Is the only gift that she'll accept.

Beware October,
Whose scythe is keenest. The old crone
Makes the earth tremble and moan.
    She's mean and won't be mocked.

Beware November,
Whose teeth are sharpened on cemetery stones,
Who will trip you up and crunch your bones.
Iron fist in iron glove.

Beware December,
False beard that hides a sneer.
Child-hater. In what year
Will we know peace?

A Crocodile in the City

The crocodile said to the cockatoo:
Cockatoo,
A croc's gotta do
What he's gotta do

The crocodile said to the chimpanzee:
Chimpanzee,
I want to be free
The jungle jangles not for me

The crocodile said to the mosquito:
Mosquito,
I must quit, oh,
I must admit, I just must go

The crocodile said to the koala bear:
Koala bear,
What are you doing up there?
You should be in Australia

The crocodile said to the parakeet:
Parakeet,
I'm stifled by this steamy heat
How I long to loll on a stone-cold street

The crocodile said to the alligator:
Alligator,
À l'heure, alligator, mate,
See you at a later date

The crocodile said to the piranha:
Piranha,
I leave for London *mañana*
Disguised as a giant banana

The crocodile said to the hippopotamus:
Sharon,
Give my love to Karen,
Gary, Wayne and Darren

Dear Mother

London cold Earth hard
Buildings giant into sky

To and fro menwo scarry
as if time on fire

At great noise cars speed
trailing bad breath

Crocodile keep to gutter
where slidder undisturbed

Dear Mother

Prisons underground
for rats are many found

Cats and dogs cowed
kowtow to menwo

Birds are not radiant
nor celebrate lives in song

Are pavement-coloured
and scream

Dear Mother

During daylight sightsee See
sights for sore eyes

See eyesores soar
So far have sightseen

Buckingham Palace Tower
Bridge Houses of Parliament

Yesterday went to Madame Tussaud's
and ate lots of famous people

Dear Mother

Night is best Moonlight
become crocodile

Stars dance in scales
asa hunting go

Late home-returner
beware puddle that move

Beware reflection that salivate
Moonlight that become crocodile

Dear Mother

Arched in pain
on pavement

Throat dry
as parchment

Parched
thirst saharan

Water water
sting of carbreath

Dear Mother

London hard Earth cold
Too tired now to hunt meat

Eat Coke cans McDonald's cartons
Kentucky fried chicken boxes

Water is black Like swallowing
putrid snake Cannot see

Tongue is swollen Head is burning
Tomorrow crocodile return home

Kentucky fried snake

Home is cold carton

chicken is swollen water

mother is putrid meat

    earth is dear

    Coke is hard

McDonald's is tired now

    head is black box

    tongue is swallowing

    London is burning

crocodile cannot see

                      tomorrow

Also by Roger McGough

Watchwords
After the Merrymaking
Gig
Sporting Relations
In the Glassroom
Unlucky for Some
Summer with Monika
Holiday on Death Row
Waving at Trains

FOR CHILDREN

The Great Smile Robbery
Sky in the Pie
Noah's Ark
The Stowaways